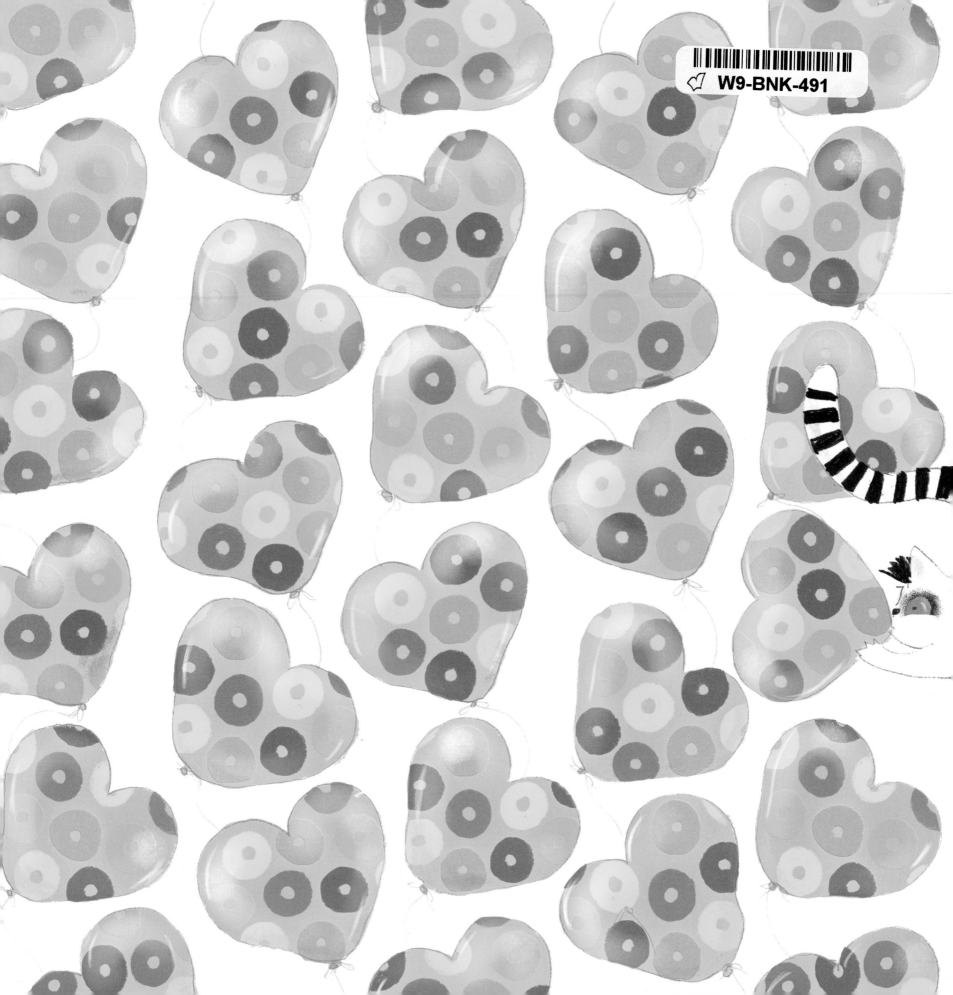

For Richard and Gabrielė

Library of Congress Cataloging-in-Publication Data available

ISBN 978-1-338-66808-7

10 9 8 7 6 5 4 3 2 1   20 21 22 23 24

Printed in China 38
This edition first printing, September 2020

The drawings in this book were created with pencils and graphite sticks. Because of his red-green
color blindness, Steve Antony usually sticks to a limited or abstract color palette.

We Love You, Mr. Panda

Steve Antony

Scholastic Press • New York

FREE
HUGS

I need a hug.

OK, Skunk. Let's have a hug.

I love you, too.

I was talking to Croc.
I love you, Croc.

May I please have a hug?

OK, Elephant. Let's have a hug.

I was talking to Mouse. I love you, Mouse.

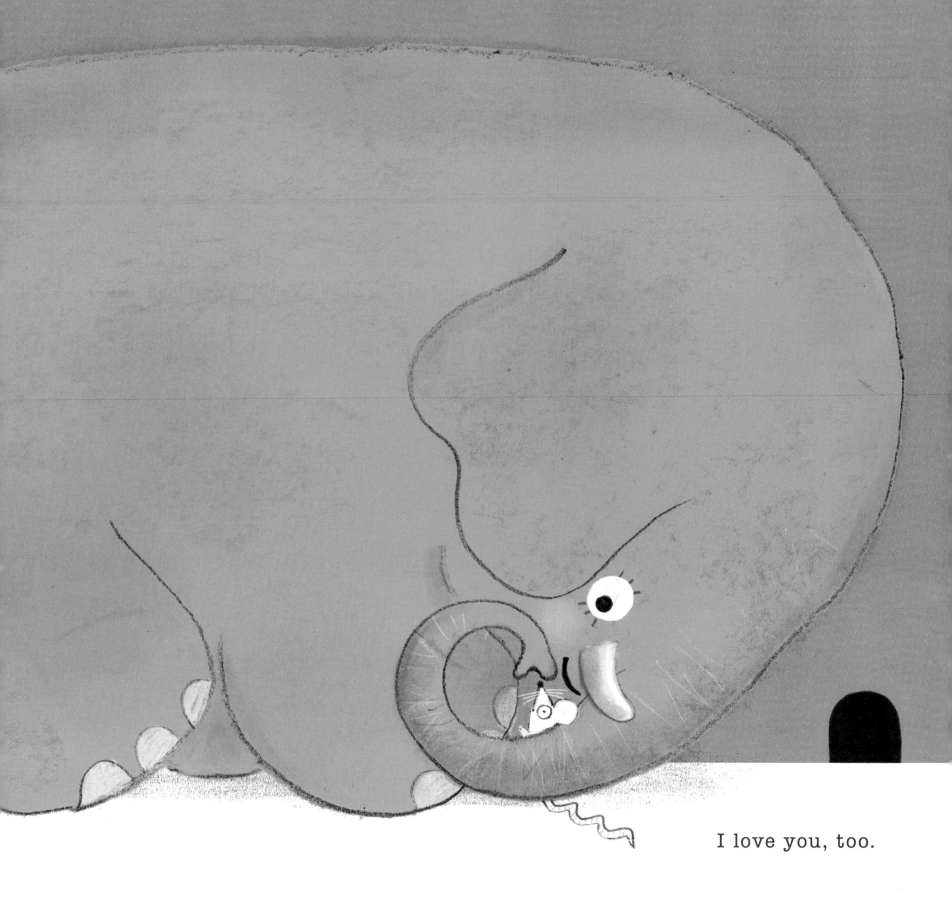

I love you, too.

Would you like a hug, Sloth?

No thanks, Mr. Panda.
I can hug myself.

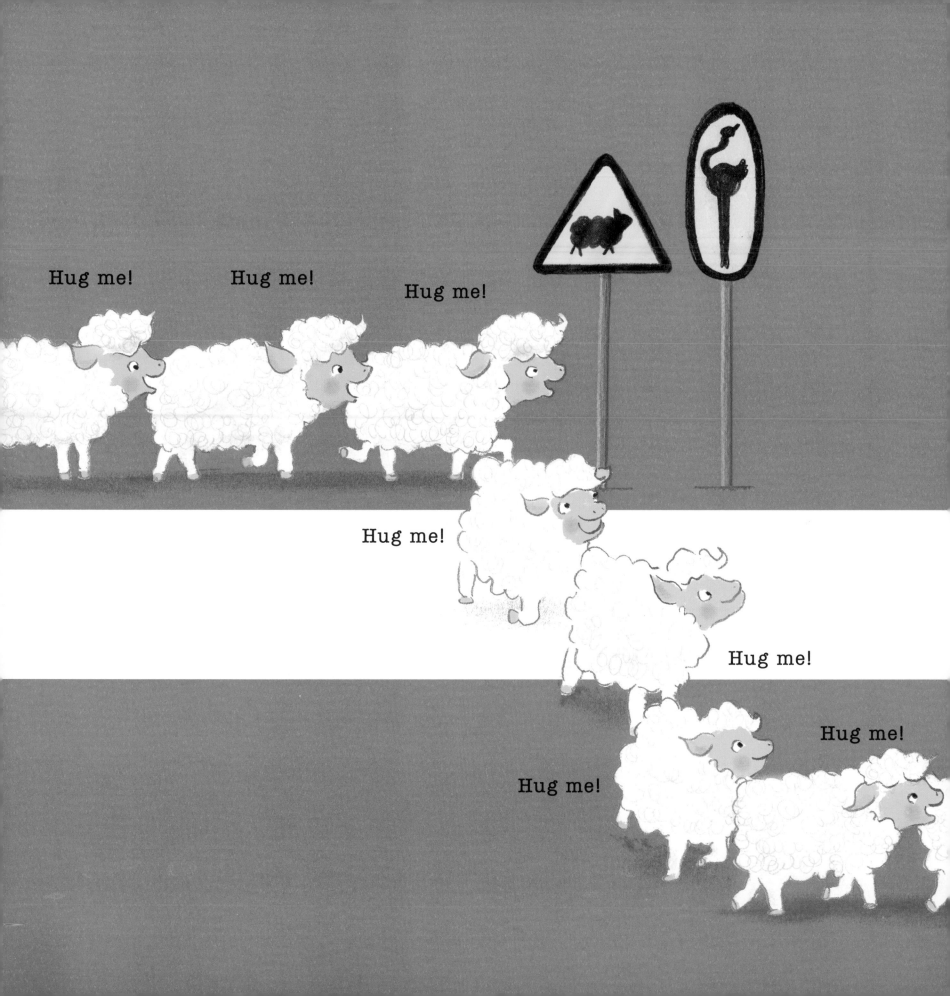

OK, sheep. Let's have a hug.

FREE HUGS

Hug me! Hug me! Hug me! Hug me! Hug me! Hug

We were talking to Ostrich.
We love you, Ostrich.

I love you all, too.

I guess nobody

wants my hugs . . .

Don't go, Mr. Panda.

Would YOU like a hug?

No, I would not like a hug . . .

. . . I would LOVE a hug. Thank you.

And so would we!

We love you, Mr. Panda!

I love you, too.